Little Wing Learns to Fly

Copyright © 2016 by HarperCollins Publishers

All rights reserved. Manufactured in China.

No part of this book may be used or reproduced in any manner whatsoever without written permission except in the case of brief quotations embodied in critical articles and reviews. For information address HarperCollins Children's Books, a division of HarperCollins Publishers, 195 Broadway, New York, NY 10007.

www.harpercollinschildrens.com

ISBN 978-0-06-236033-5

The artist used pencils, watercolors, and Adobe Photoshop to create the digital illustrations for this book.

Book design by Victor Joseph Ochoa

16 17 18 19 20   SCP   10 9 8 7 6 5 4 3 2 1

❖

First Edition

Little Wing

Learns to Fly

by **Calista Brill**

illustrated by **Jennifer A. Bell**

HARPER

An Imprint of HarperCollinsPublishers

"Today's the day," I told my mama. "Today I'm going to fly."
"Just be careful, Little Wing," Mama said. "You don't want to get hurt . . . again."

Flying isn't easy, even for a dragon like me.
But a dragon never gives up. So I practiced hard every day.
And every day, it was the same:

Flip.

Flap.

Flop . . .

Jumping off the top step . . .

Flip.

Flap.

Flop . . .

But like I said, a dragon never gives up.
Today was going to be different. I just knew it.
"Watch me, Mama!" I said. "Watch!"

Flip.

Flap.

Flop . . .

"Next time," Mama said. "That's enough for today."
"Wait," I said. "A dragon never gives up!"

I stood still. I squeezed my eyes shut tight. And . . .

Flip.

Flap.

Flutter!

"You're doing it!" Mama said.
"I'm doing it!" I yelled.

I was *flip!*

Flap!

FLYING!

Everything looked so different from above.
"Come down, Little Wing," Mama said.
"Why?" I asked.
"There are rules about flying," Mama said.

"Rules?" I said.
I thought up a good rule.
"A dragon never comes down!"

"Rule number one," Mama said.
"Don't fly too high!"
  "But how high is too high?" I said.
"Is this too high?"

"Rule number two," Mama said. "Don't fly too far!"

"But how far is too far?" I said. I let the wind carry me to the edge of the yard. "Is this too far?"

"Rule number three," Mama said. "Don't fly without me. . . ."

But I could barely hear her by then. The wind caught my wings and carried me out over the forest.

The wind pushed and pulled. It bumped me up when I tried to go down. It sent me right when I wanted to go left. Soon I couldn't even see my house anymore!

A dragon never lies.

I was **flip.**

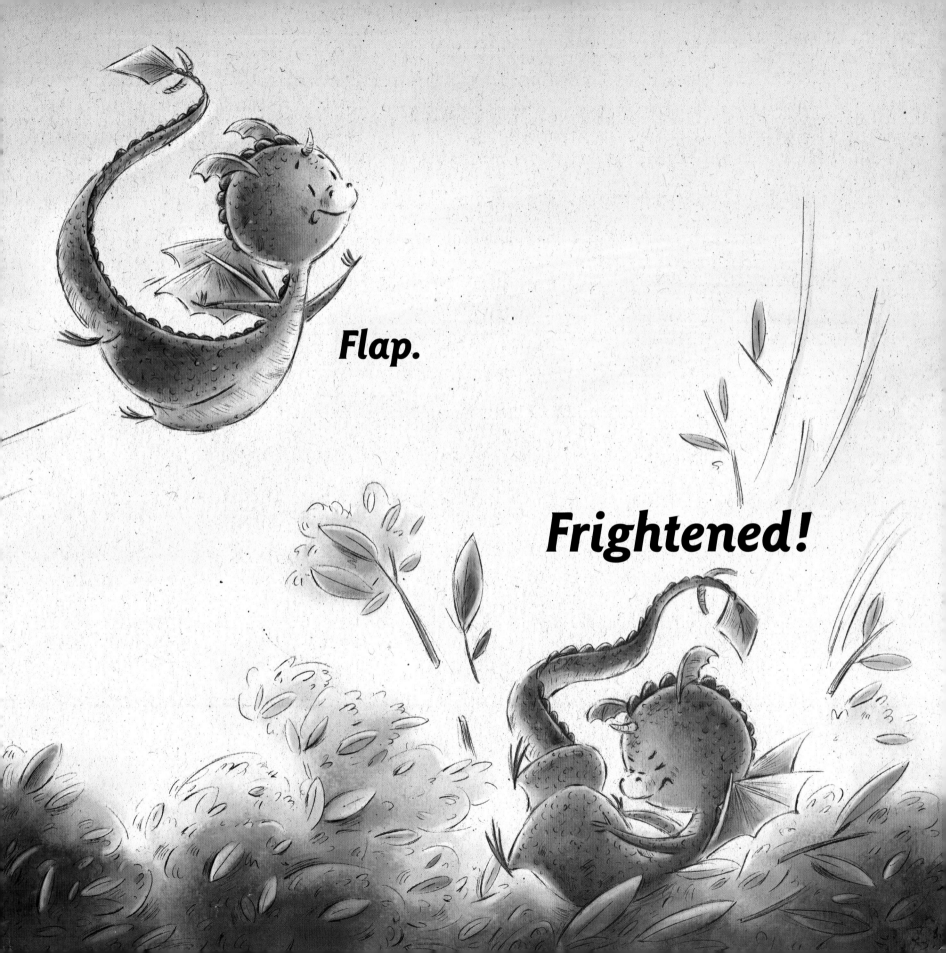

Flap.

Frightened!

Finally I snagged my tail around the tip-tip-top of a tall, tall tree. I climbed down to the ground. *Whew.*

But where was I? Where was
my house? Where was my mama?
What was I going to do?

"Mama!" I yelled as loudly
as I could. *"Mama!"*

"MAMA!"

"You found me!"
"Of course I did!" my mama said. "A dragon never gives up."

"So," Mama said. "About those rules."
"One," I said. "Don't fly too high."
"Two?" she asked.
I told her, "Don't fly too far."
"Three," she said. "Promise you won't fly without me."
"I won't."

And a dragon always
keeps his promises.

It was a long way home.
But with my mama close
behind me, I was . . .

Flip.

Flap.

FEARLESS!